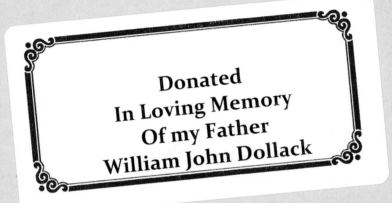

SMUDGE BUNNY

by Dr. Bernie Siegel
Illustrated by Laura J. Bryant

H J KRAMER
STARSEED PRESS
TIBURON, CALIFORNIA

For my wife, Bobbie, our beloved grandchildren,
dear Smudge, and all the other animals and
children, who by their completeness teach
us about the meaning of love.
B. S.

For my dad.
L. J. B.

Art Director: Linda Kramer
Design and production: Jan Phillips, San Anselmo, California

Library of Congress Cataloging-in-Publication Data

Siegel, Bernie S.
  Smudge Bunny / by Bernie Siegel ; illustrated by Laura J. Bryant.
      p.   cm.
  Summary: When two little rabbits, sisters named Smudge and
Snowflake, are taken from their barn and endure some difficult days,
they still try to believe that "troubles can turn into blessings."
  ISBN 1-932073-03-5 (alk. paper)
  [1. Optimism—Fiction. 2. Rabbits—Fiction. 3. Sisters—Fiction.] I.
Bryant, Laura J., ill. II. Title.
PZ7.S56653 Sm 2003
[E]—dc22   2003017729

H J Kramer
Starseed Press
P.O. Box 1082
Tiburon, California 94920

Printed in Singapore

10 9 8 7 6 5 4 3 2 1

PREFACE

Smudge Bunny is a true story about our beloved pet rabbit and her journey to reach our home and family. Since my wife, Bobbie, and I found Smudge, our lives have been full of interesting experiences and opportunities for learning. Some of the lessons have been painful.

I had always wanted a dog. One day, while visiting the animal shelter, I saw a cute little Lhasa apso who was attracted to me. I spoke to my wife about the possibility of adopting him. "We don't need another furphy in our lives," she answered. I laughed because my wife is always coming up with new words and names for animals.

The next day that little dog was still at the shelter. I felt he was my Furphy and that his destiny was to go home with me. My wife has a warm heart, and after she took one look at him I knew that we were in.

I talked to several veterinarians about how to introduce Furphy to our four cats and Smudge. Well, the cats knew how to threaten him. They sat in front of the pet door hissing, and he was afraid to come back into the house without my help. Smudge, however, is not a predator and had no way to threaten a dog except to thump on the ground and make scary grunting sounds. Furphy treated Smudge like a stuffed toy, and Bobbie or I would scold him and explain that we were all family.

Things seemed to be working out until the day we left the house for an hour to shop, and I forgot to close the pet door. Out came Furphy and almost shook the life out of Smudge. When we came home we found Smudge in her house, bruised and listless. I cleaned up her wounds and watched her carefully. When she didn't eat, I spoon-fed her and gave her fluids. The next day I took her to the vet.

She needed antibiotics, nutritional support, more fluids, and surgery for her wounds and infections. She hurt so much she couldn't chew. I was in tears, and I still cry when I think about this, knowing it was my fault for leaving the pet door open. At home I made a special soft food for Smudge, continued to spoon-feed her, dressed her wounds, and gave her antibiotics. Even though she was my only patient, I was very busy for weeks. She is healing now, and Furphy is still a family member.

Every night I hold Smudge to show how much I love her and to show Furphy we are family. I know she has forgiven me and Furphy, too. No person is as forgiving as animals are, and as a doctor I know you can't cure everything. But you can help people heal their lives. It is painful when your actions hurt someone you love, but I also know how forgiving loved ones can be when you admit your mistakes and say, "I'm sorry." Love and forgiveness heal lives. It is simpler for animals than people.

Once upon a time, in a big old drafty barn, a mother bunny gave birth to six little bunnies. Every day she would cuddle her babies to keep them warm and cozy. Even thunderstorms didn't seem scary because her hugs made them feel safe.

When they were old enough to understand, Momma Bunny announced, "Today I'm going to give each of you a name."

She looked at her biggest baby who had soft coal-black fur and said, "Smudge would be a good name for you."

She then turned to Smudge's favorite sister, "And you are Snowflake." Pointing to the others Momma declared, "You are Missy, Barney, Sybil, and you, you little rascal, are Dickens."

As they grew stronger, Momma's babies began to hop
around the barn. They loved playing hide-and-seek
in the straw. Smudge would always win because
she could disappear in the shadows.
Sometimes they would play tag
or race around the barnyard
to see who was the fastest.

Other times they would get lost or stuck in tight places and cry for Momma.

Momma Bunny would always find and comfort them. "Don't be afraid when life seems difficult or frightening," she'd say. "Sometimes our troubles turn out to be blessings, and we can learn many things from them."

Momma's words always made the bunnies feel better.

When the bunnies were six weeks old, the farmer and his wife entered the barn carrying a big box. The bunnies were excited, thinking the box was for a new game. Momma Bunny knew better. She remembered the day that Poppa Bunny was taken away in a box like that. He had never returned to the barn. She tried to hide her babies, but they kept sticking their noses out to see what was happening.

"Let's take the chubby black one and the little white one," said the woman. "They make a cute pair. I'm sure the pet store will want them."

Momma Bunny nuzzled Smudge and Snowflake. "Don't be afraid," she whispered. "Remember, something good will come of this."

When Smudge and Snowflake arrived at the pet shop, a lady gently placed them in a cage in the front window. They were surrounded by squawking birds, barking dogs, and meowing kittens. They missed their mother, brothers, and sisters, but Momma's words brought them comfort and hope.

The days passed slowly. Children would come and stare at Smudge and Snowflake, pointing excitedly. One little boy reached into the cage and picked Smudge up by the ears, making her cry.

One afternoon, an older couple came into the store. "Gramps," said the woman, "these two would make cute Easter bunnies for Ashley."

"Honey, that's a great idea. We'll put them in the empty hamster cage."

Before they knew what was happening, the bunnies found themselves in a small wire cage with no room to play. Whenever they moved, they bumped into their water dish or knocked over their food bowl.

Early that evening, Ashley and her parents came to visit. "Look at the Easter bunnies!" she cried excitedly.

She grabbed Smudge by the fur on her back. Smudge felt herself slipping from Ashley's small hands. Her long ears wiggled as she fearfully kicked the air trying to hold on. Her nails, long and sharp from having spent too much time in a cage, scratched Ashley's arm as she fell.

"Ouch!" Ashley cried. "You made me bleed. You're a bad bunny!"

Ashley's grandmother was very upset. She put Smudge back in the cage while Ashley's parents cleaned and bandaged the scratch. Then she carried the cage into the backyard and dumped the bunnies onto the grass. "Shoo, you little troublemakers," she hissed.

Smudge and Snowflake hopped around the yard searching for a place to hide. "Who will take care of us now?" Snowflake asked as she sniffed the air trying to decide what to do next.

The two frightened bunnies hid beneath a bush. Smudge lay down in front of Snowflake to protect her. When the sun set, it grew chilly and the neighbors' barking dogs frightened them. Smudge tried to comfort Snowflake. "Remember what Momma always said. This will lead to something good." Snowflake wasn't sure she could believe Momma anymore.

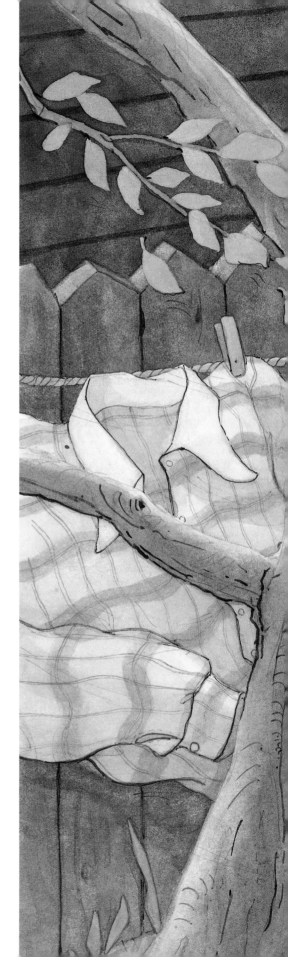

The next morning the hungry bunnies left their hiding place and hopped through a hole in the fence to look for food. As they did, they heard a woman's voice. "Come here little bunnies. We have dandelion leaves and a nutty nut for you."

Smudge began to move towards the man and woman who were calling to them. Snowflake stopped her.

"I don't want to end up in another cage," she warned.

That night Smudge and Snowflake stayed in the friendly couple's yard. Smudge dug a hole for them to hide in.

When Snowflake fell asleep Smudge hopped over to the porch where the couple had left some food and water before going to bed.

When she finished eating, she hopped back to tell Snowflake the good news, but Snowflake was gone.

Smudge's heart was broken. She crawled into her hole and tried to believe what Momma had said.

When Smudge woke up the next morning, there was a cage filled with rabbit treats sitting in the yard. She looked around carefully. It looked safe so she hopped inside. As soon as she touched the food, the cage door snapped shut.

"Don't be scared, little bunny. You're safe now," the lady promised as she gently picked Smudge up and carried her into the warm house.

Once inside, she handed the bunny to her husband. He cradled Smudge and spoke in a soft voice. "Nice little bunny. Where's your little white friend?" He gently petted her belly. "Why, you look like a sweet little Smudge Bunny." At the sound of her name, she relaxed. Feeling comfortable and safe, Smudge began to get drowsy.

The last thing she remembered before drifting off to sleep was her new dad saying, "I'm going to build Smudge her very own house."

The next day, Smudge's new mom and dad, Bobbie and Bernie, took her out to the yard. There stood the greatest little house a rabbit could ever want. It had a bedroom, a kitchen with timothy hay and a touch of alfalfa, a bathroom filled with soft litter, and a heater for cold nights.

When Smudge seemed comfortable in her new home, Bobbie and Bernie introduced her to their four cats. Her new brothers and sisters did not enjoy playing nose tag, so she often got a thwack on the head when she charged up to nuzzle them. She had to learn they weren't bunnies.

At first Smudge was frightened by strangers and loud noises and would jump into her litter box to hide. Every night after dinner, Bernie would hold Smudge in his arms and rub her tummy. Sometimes he would lie on the floor, and she would nap on his chest.

At bedtime she would play tag with Bobbie and Bernie and make them chase her around the living room furniture.

Smudge was grateful for her new family, but she missed Snowflake and couldn't stop thinking about her.

One sunny afternoon, Bobbie and Bernie went out to the
yard with a leash and a harness. "Smudge, guess what?
Today, little sweetness, you're going to join us for a walk."

Smudge was excited to be going out with her parents, and
she stood very still while they put her harness on. She
hopped right along between them as they started out.

Bobbie, Bernie, and Smudge were having a great time
when they reached the bottom of their long driveway.
There in front of them was a big sign stapled to a tree.
It said FOUND BUNNY with a nearby address.

Bobbie and Bernie looked at each other. Could this be the white rabbit they had seen with Smudge? Bobbie picked Smudge up, hurried down the street to the address listed, and rang the bell. When a lady answered, Bobbie asked, "Could we see the rabbit you found? Is it white?"

"Well," said the lady, "she might have been white once, but she's a bit bedraggled at the moment. Let me get her."

The lady returned with the bunny in her arms. It was Snowflake! Smudge was overjoyed and grunted happily as Bobbie put her on the ground. She hopped over and rubbed noses with her sister. Snowflake's little heart felt like it would burst with happiness.

The first thing Bernie did when they got home was give Snowflake a bath. When she was dry and sweet smelling, he carried her to Smudge's house, where Bobbie served them a special meal of fresh greens and walnuts. After eating, the sisters cuddled together in the soft hay, just as they had in the barn with Momma. Before they fell asleep Smudge heard Snowflake whisper, "Momma was right — troubles can turn into blessings. I guess you just have to believe."

Caring for House Rabbits

1. If you acquire a rabbit, be prepared to give it as much time and care as you would a dog or cat.

2. Rabbits, if spayed or neutered, have a lifespan of seven to ten years. Spaying and neutering are simple operations that tend to reduce or prevent territorial behavior, spraying by males, moodiness, aggressiveness, digging, and chewing. They can also improve litter box habits.

3. Brush your rabbit regularly to avoid fur balls, which they may swallow but cannot regurgitate.

4. To keep their teeth healthy, rabbits need hard items to chew on. Bunny-proof your home to protect wires and furniture, and provide the rabbit with plenty of chewable items.

5. Rabbits are afraid of predators, and they can literally be scared to death. So when you pick up a rabbit, hold it securely so it feels safe. The reason many people, especially children, get scratched by rabbits is that they don't hold them properly.

6. Rabbits should generally be kept indoors and supervised while outdoors because the outside world is a dangerous place for them. If given the opportunity, they may dig up your yard and eat the flowers and plants.

7. Rabbits, by nature, are clean and neat. They can also be affectionate and social, intelligent and sensitive, playful, curious, and mischievous. Many rabbits get along with cats and dogs, but the animals involved need to be trained, and you should closely supervise early interactions between rabbits and other pets.

8. Be sure to find a veterinarian who is trained in rabbit care, as rabbits are considered exotic pets.

For more information, visit the house rabbit web site, www.houserabbit.org.